bendon®

Bendon, Inc. All rights reserved.
The BENDON name, logo, and Tear and Share are
trademarks of Bendon, Inc. Ashland, OH 44805.

Come on, everyone! All paws on deck!

HERE COMES RUBBLE ON THE DOUBLE!

RYDER

CHASE

MARSHALL

RUBBLE

SKYE

EVEREST

Time to protect the citizens of Adventure Bay.

HOW MANY WORDS

How many words can you make using the letters in:

ADVENTURE BAY

_____

_____

_____

_____

_____

_____

_____

_____

_____

_____

We're here to help!

Let's roll!

BADGE MATCH

Match each badge to the right PAW Patrol pup.

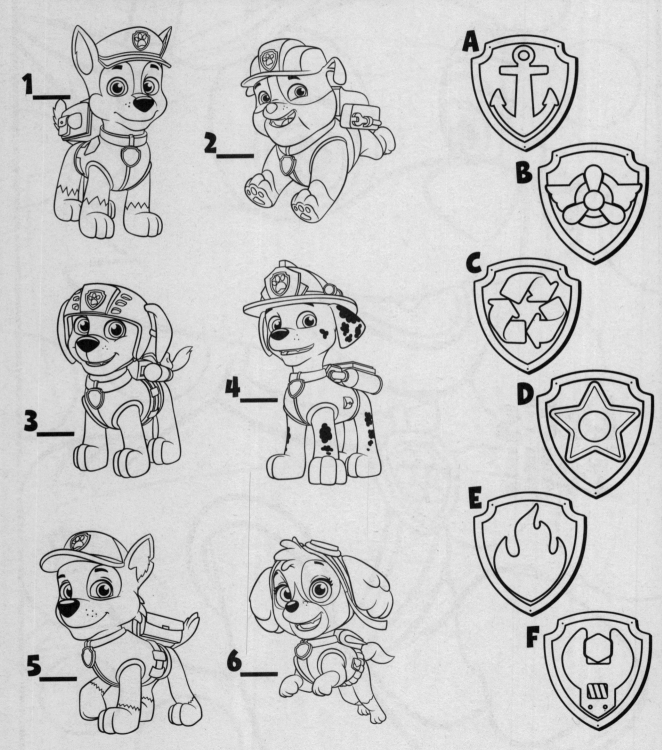

1___

2___

3___

4___

5___

6___

A

B

C

D

E

F

DESIGN YOUR OWN
PAW PATROL BADGE!

Write your name here.

LET'S DRAW!

Use the grid to draw Everest.

Looks like there's a new pup in town!

LET'S DRAW!

Use the grid to draw Marshall.

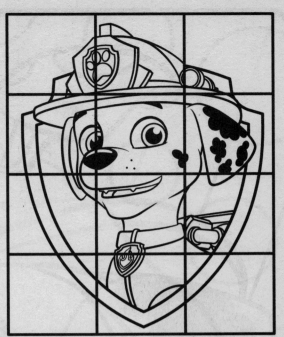

WORD JUMBLE

Put the letters in the right order to reveal one of Rubble's favorite phrases.

TSEL IDG TI

_ _ _ _ ' _   _ _ _   _ _ _!

WORD SEARCH

Zuma wants to play!

Look up, down, and across for these words:

BONE TOYS BALL CHEW

PLAY PULL DIG RUN CATCH

M D B R L G T
O T O U P E A
D E N N L O Y
C H E W A K T
A G T O Y S P
T E S T E U U
C K R B A L L
H D I G M N L

A-MAZE-ING!

Help Skye take to the sky!

FINISH

START

Everest and Skye have some girl time.

SHADOW MATCH

Which shadow matches Chase?

A

B

C

SHADOW MATCH

Which shadow matches Rubble?

A

B

C

WORD SEARCH

Look up, down, and across for these words.

SKYE   RUBBLE   EVEREST
CHASE   ZUMA   MARSHALL
ROCKY   RYDER

```
Z U M A H N S
E C A E J K C
V H R Y D E R
E A S O N R U
R S H I D O B
E E A L Y C B
S R L D H K L
T B L S K Y E
```

COUNT IT UP

How many paw prints do you count? Answer: _____

LET'S DRAW!

Use the grid to draw Ryder.

Pups in Action

HOW MANY?

How many tennis balls do you see? Answer: _____

How many bones? Answer: _____

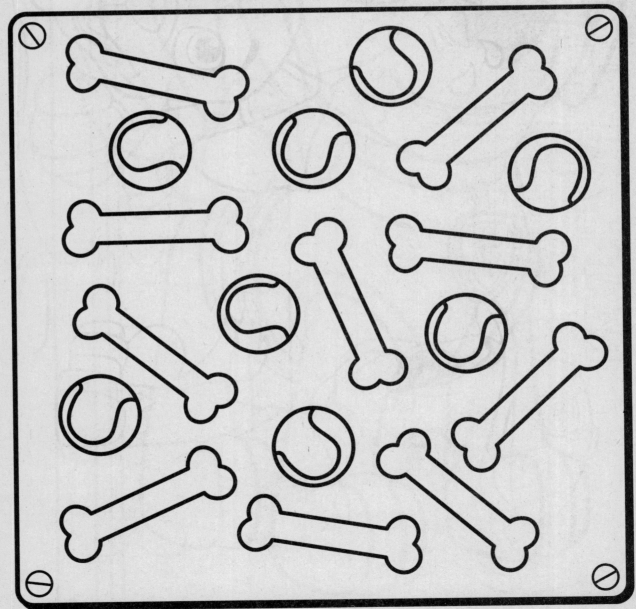

WHICH PATH?

Which path leads Rubble to his bulldozer?

A

B

C

WHICH IS DIFFERENT?

Which Everest is different from the others?

LET'S DRAW!

Use the grid to draw Chase.

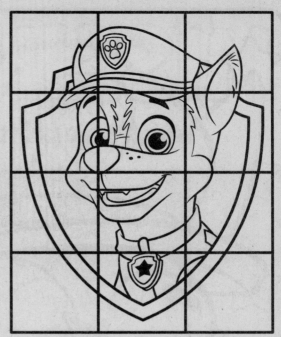

MISSING PIECE

Which paw print completes the picture?

A

B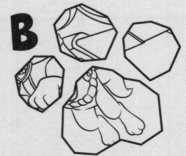

C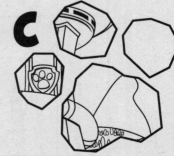

Answer: B

WORD JUMBLE

Put the letters in the right order to reveal one of Zuma's favorite phrases.

SETL IVED NI

____ ___ , ____ ____ ___!

SPIRAL MAZE

Help Rocky get to the ball.

START

Why trash it when you can stash it?

RHYME TIME

How many words can you think of that rhyme with PACK?

_____

_____

_____

_____

_____

_____

SORT IT OUT

These fire hoses are all tangled! Follow the path of each fire hose to see which one is which.

A   B   C

1___   2___   3___

WHICH PATH?

Which path leads Chase to the ball?

A

B

C

WHICH IS DIFFERENT?

Which Zuma is different from the others?

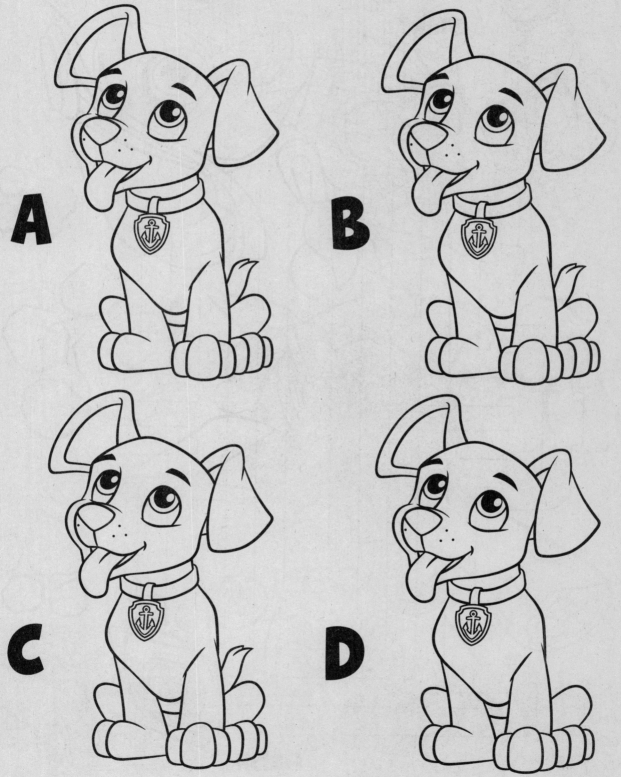

A-MAZE-ING!

Help Marshall get to his fire engine!

START

FINISH

SHADOW MATCH

Which shadow matches Chase?

A

B

C

RHYME TIME

How many words can you think of that rhyme with ROLL?

_____

_____

_____

_____

_____

_____

_____

HOW MANY WORDS

How many words can you make using the letters in:

TO THE RESCUE

_____

_____

_____

_____

_____

_____

_____

_____

On the Scene

WHICH IS DIFFERENT?

Which Zuma is different from the others?

CHASE

LET'S DRAW!

Use the grid to draw Chase.

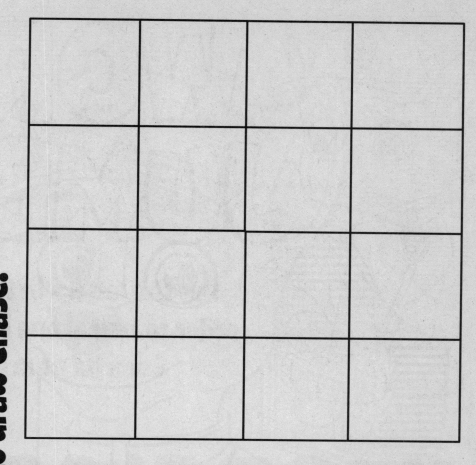

WORD JUMBLE

Put the letters in the right order to reveal one of Rocky's favorite phrases.

NODT ELSO TI

,

_ _ _ _ _ _ _ _

SEERU TI

!

_ _ _ _ _ _

ROCKY

ZUMA

A-MAZE-ING!

Help Zuma find the bone.

START

FINISH

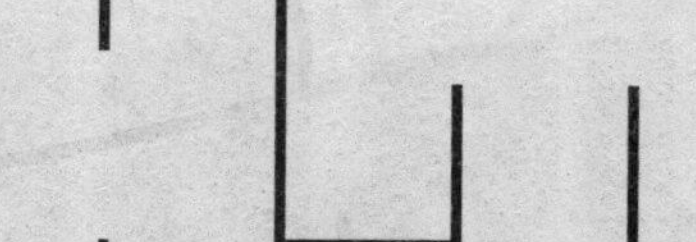

WORD SEARCH

Look up, down, and across for these words.

PUPPY   BALL   PAW
BONE   PLAY   YELP
PATROL

```
G P A T R O L L
R U M C T B T
R P O B M O E
F P R A C N H
M Y E L P E M
H C G L A B K
J T F H W Y N
P L A Y G K F
```

MARSHALL

HOW MANY WORDS

How many words can you make using the letters in:

JUST YELP FOR HELP

_____

_____

_____

_____

_____

_____

_____

_____

_____

_____

My nose knows!

MISSING PIECE

Which paw print completes the picture?

A

B

C

WHICH IS DIFFERENT?

Which Rocky is different from the others?

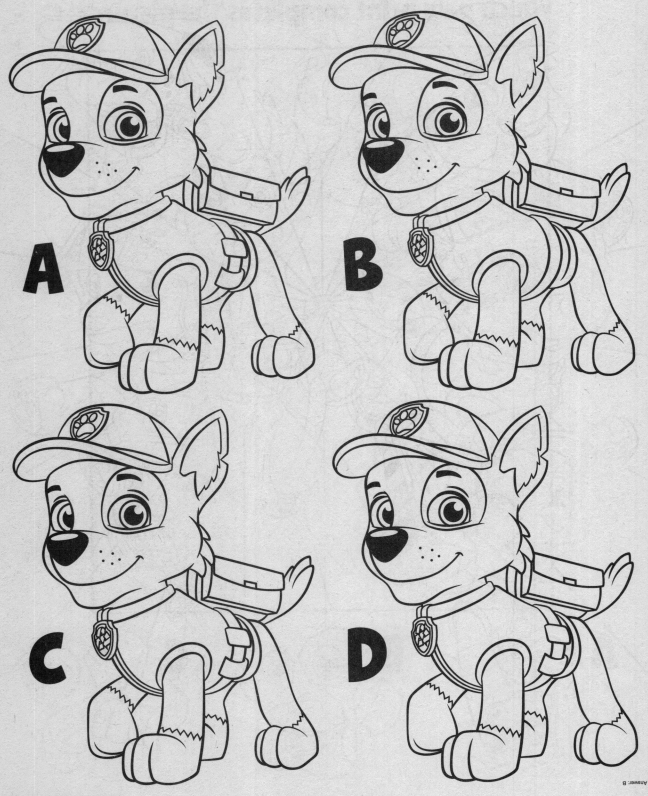

A

B

C

D

Answer: B

PUPS AWAY!

NO JOB TOO BIG, NO PUP TOO SMALL!